The First Franklin Christmas Tree

Story by Professor Thadamouse
Illustrated by Claudie C. Bergeron
Professor Thadamouse Illustrated by Tim Parker

ISBN: 978-1-7370547-0-2 (Hardcover)
ISBN: 978-1-7370547-1-9 (Paperback)
Also available in Kindle ebook format

Design and layout by Lighthouse24

VALIANTMOUSE

For Cathy and Benjamin.

And for every kid, from one to ninety-two.

There is a Magic deeper still.

Once, not long ago, when the world was a just a bit younger than it is now, the little town of Franklin was born. The people who lived there were so very loving and neighborly that even strangers passing through were welcomed with great kindness.

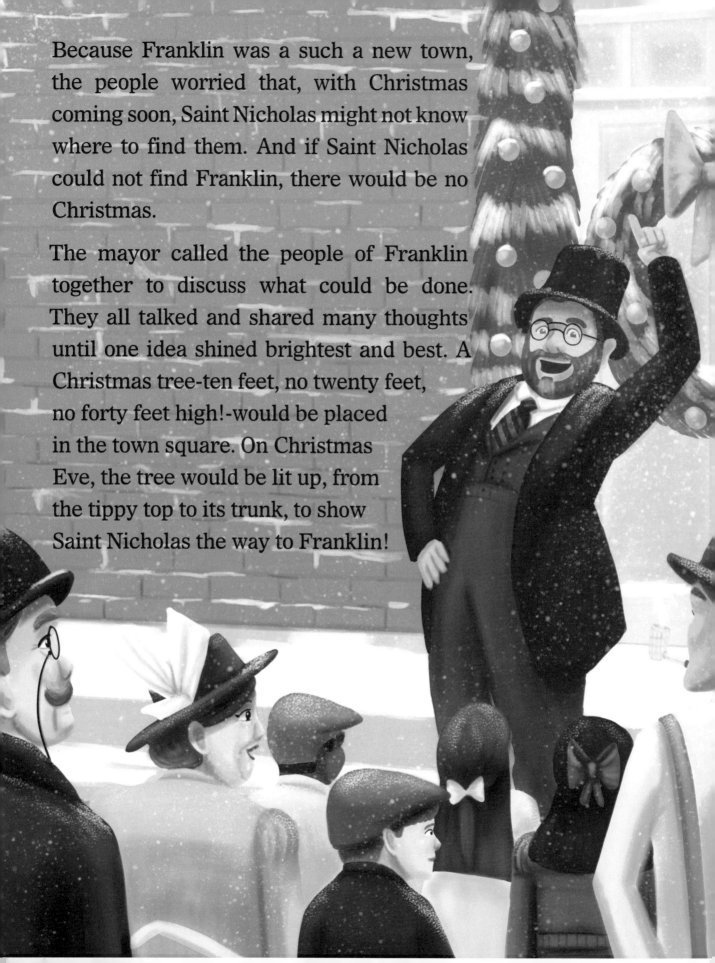

Because Franklin was a such a new town, the people worried that, with Christmas coming soon, Saint Nicholas might not know where to find them. And if Saint Nicholas could not find Franklin, there would be no Christmas.

The mayor called the people of Franklin together to discuss what could be done. They all talked and shared many thoughts until one idea shined brightest and best. A Christmas tree-ten feet, no twenty feet, no forty feet high!-would be placed in the town square. On Christmas Eve, the tree would be lit up, from the tippy top to its trunk, to show Saint Nicholas the way to Franklin!

In the forest at the edge of town the people found a beautiful evergreen tree that was ten feet, no **twenty feet**, no **FORTY FEET** high!

They placed the tree in the town square and covered it with candles from the tippy top to its trunk.

Go to **http://www.professorthadamouse.com** where you can...

 Learn more fun facts about Professor Thadamouse at his home in the hollow of the Great Oak Tree

 Sign up for the Professor's mailing list and receive #4 free coloring pages that you can download

 By signing up on the Professor's mailing list you will also receive his newsletter, ***Happenings from the Hollow***.

 Find other fun items and gifts in the Professor's online store.

(If you are under age 13, you must ask a grown-up to sign up for you, or you must get a grown-up's permission to sign up for the Professor's mailing list.)

Please Leave a Review
Authors love hearing from readers!

Please let Professor Thadamouse know what you thought about *The First Franklin Christmas Tree*, by leaving a short review on Amazon or your other preferred online store. It will help other parents and children find the story.

(If you are under age 13, ask a grown-up to help you)

Thank you!

CPSIA information can be obtained
at www.ICGtesting.com
Printed in the USA
BVRC091002140921
616730BV00007B/172

9 781737 054702

So beautiful and bright was the first Franklin Christmas Tree that on Christmas Eve Saint Nicholas saw the tree shining like a diamond in the night. Turning his sleigh toward the town, the jolly old man visited each and every home that first Franklin Christmas.

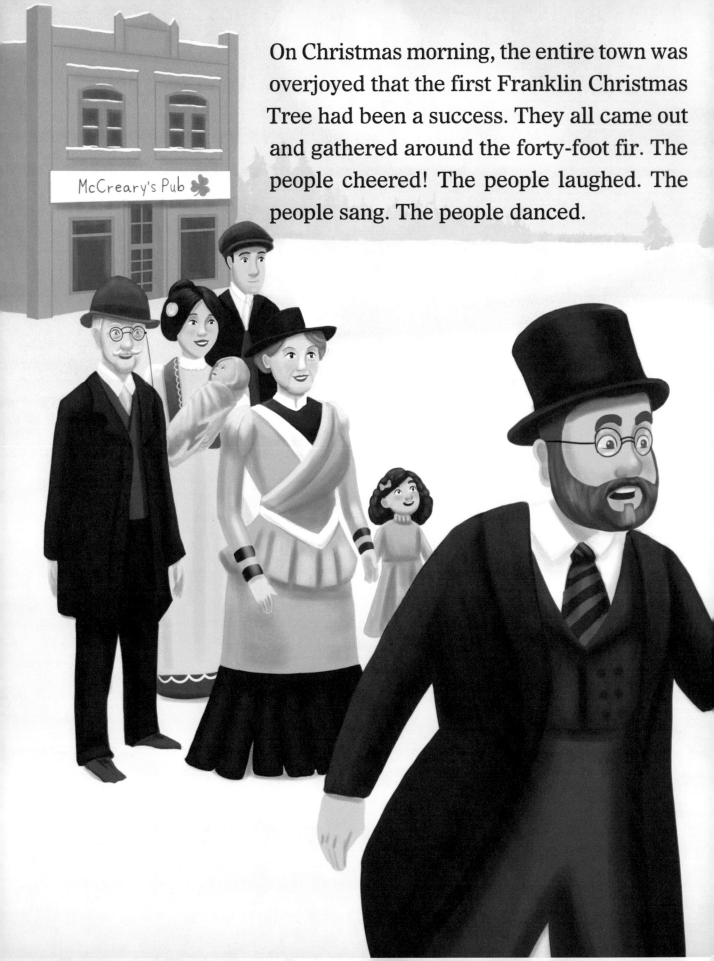

On Christmas morning, the entire town was overjoyed that the first Franklin Christmas Tree had been a success. They all came out and gathered around the forty-foot fir. The people cheered! The people laughed. The people sang. The people danced.

Amidst the celebration, the mayor noticed a parchment, rolled up and tied to one of the branches with a velvet green ribbon. It was a letter from Saint Nicholas himself!

The mayor read aloud:

O, Little Town of Franklin,

Merry Christmas! What wonderful Christmas spirit you all have! The glow of the first Franklin Christmas Tree shined big and bright through the night. But even bigger and brighter still is the love you have for each other. It is because you worked together, as family, friends, and neighbors all, that I was able to find my way to your new town.

This love you have is what Christmas is truly all about. And because of this, I have one more gift to give you, which you will find under the first Franklin Christmas Tree on New Year's Eve at the stroke of midnight.

Merry and Bright on this
Frosty Christmas Morning,

Saint Nicholas

The town was overjoyed. And on New Year's Eve, the people gathered once more around the first Franklin Christmas Tree to ring in the New Year. Remembering stories of the past year, and wondering what the new year might bring, they waited with hopeful hearts.

Finally, the church bells rang out at the stroke of midnight, and a hush fell over the town square. The light from the tree seemed to suddenly shine brighter, ablaze with beauty. The people gasped in great wonder. And just as suddenly, the light returned to its original glow. Filled with curiosity, they all moved closer to investigate.

Two treasures were found.
A pinecone, glittering with a
magic light all its own, rested
on one of the lower boughs of the
great tree. And beneath the tree lay
a small chest made of pure gold.

The mayor slowly, and solemnly, opened the golden chest. Inside were several curious objects: another parchment rolled up and tied with a velvet green ribbon, a crystal bottle filled with water and topped with a cork as red as holly berries, and a garden trowel with a red and white striped handle that looked just like a candy-cane.

Removing the parchment from the box and untying the velvet green ribbon, the mayor found a second letter from Saint Nicholas.

O, Little Town of Franklin,

Merry Eighth Day of Christmas and Happy New Year!

My final gift will continue the love you all gave to each other this first Franklin Christmas, for love is the true heart of Christmas!

This magic pinecone will carry on the love of the first Franklin Christmas Tree for many Christmases to come. Harvest this treasure from the tree and place it in the golden chest to keep until the dawning of the next Christmas season.

On November first, All Saints Day, you are to gather together. Using the candy cane-handled trowel, plant the magic pinecone in the center of the town square. Within the crystal bottle is magical, melted snow from my home in the North Pole. Once a week, water the tree until it has grown ten feet, no twenty feet, no forty feet high!

Now I give you my blessing and Merry Christmas to you all.

With Warm Laughter on this
Chilly New Year's Day,

Saint Nicholas

The townspeople, in awe of Saint Nicholas's words, watched quietly as the mayor plucked the magic pinecone and gently placed it in the golden chest next to the other treasures. The last rays of glittering light from the pinecone shined brightly as the mayor closed the golden chest. The people cheered! The people laughed. The people sang. The people danced. And then they wished their final wishes to each other for a happy new year.

Over the next several days, festivities continued with the ninth, tenth, and eleventh days of Christmas. They finished the season around the first Franklin Christmas Tree with a final celebration on Twelfth night.

The following day, the people worked together to take the Christmas Tree down from the town square, overjoyed at how wonderful their first Christmas together had been.

The new year moved on, each season having its own
place and purpose. **Springtime** brought blooming
and blossoming, as life and green returned to
the forests and meadows.

Next came
summer and with it
the growing of gardens,
climbing and swimming!

Then **autumn** and
harvest-time arrived,
kissing the town with
cooler winds and
colorful trees.

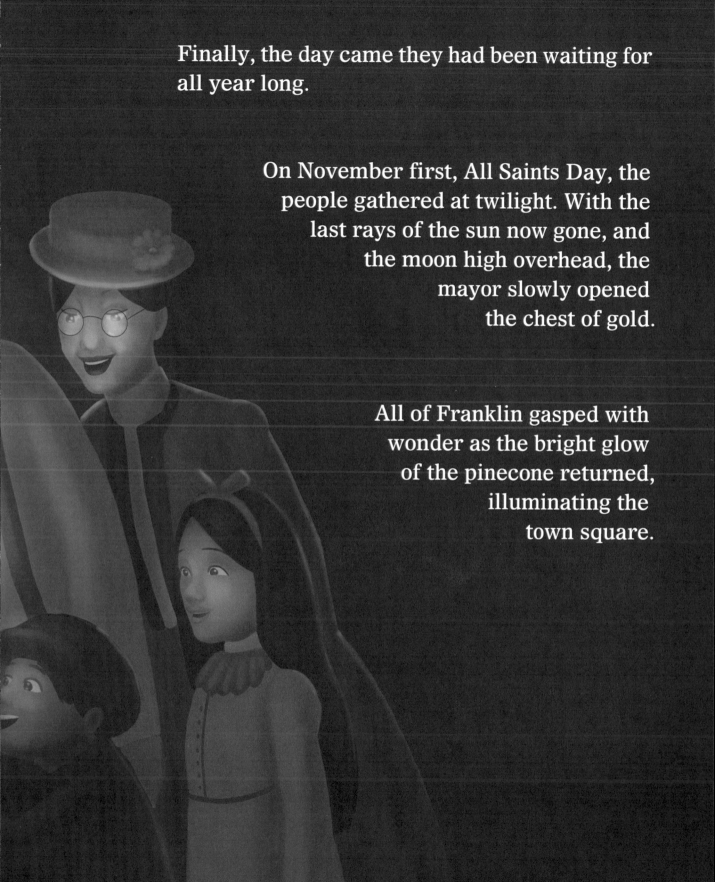

Finally, the day came they had been waiting for all year long.

On November first, All Saints Day, the people gathered at twilight. With the last rays of the sun now gone, and the moon high overhead, the mayor slowly opened the chest of gold.

All of Franklin gasped with wonder as the bright glow of the pinecone returned, illuminating the town square.

An older farmer stepped forward and, taking the candy cane-handled trowel, he dug a hole in the earth.

Next, a shopkeeper, her eyes wide with excitement, removed the glittering pinecone from the golden chest and placed it in the ground.

Finally, a child took the crystal bottle and poured the magical, melted snow from the North Pole over the buried treasure. With the last drop of water gone, the child placed the holly-berry red cork back in the bottle. And oh, wonder of wonders! The crystal bottle magically filled up with water again.

The people cheered! The people laughed.
The people sang. The people danced.

And while they were amazed by this magic, they also wondered how the tree would grow to be ten feet, no **twenty feet**, no **FORTY FEET** high! in time for Christmas.

A week went by and following Saint Nicholas's instruction, they returned to water the ground where the magic pinecone was buried. The people were amazed to find that where they had planted the glittering seed now stood a small sprig of fir tree!

Once again, a child poured out the magical, melted snow from the North Pole upon the small sprig of fir. And oh, wonder of wonders! Placing the holly-berry red cork back in the crystal bottle, it magically filled with water a second time.

Another week passed, and the people returned again to water the small sprig of fir. They were overjoyed because where the small sprig had been, there now stood a little tree, three feet high!

Taking the crystal bottle, a child poured out the magical, melted snow from the North Pole upon the three-foot fir tree. With the last drop of water gone, the child placed the holly-berry red cork back in the bottle.

But oh, puzzle of puzzles! The magical water did not fill the bottle this time. All who had assembled in the town square wondered at what this could mean. They wondered just as much as they wondered if the tree would reach ten feet, no **twenty feet**, no **FORTY FEET** high! in time for Christmas.

But just as the little tree continued to grow, so did the faith of the people of Franklin continue to grow deep inside their hearts.

Gathering together a week later, the whole town marveled at what they found. The small three-foot fir tree was now ten feet, no **twenty feet**, no **FORTY FEET** high! The people cheered! The people laughed. The people sang. The people danced.

Later that evening, with the last rays of the sun now gone and the moon high overhead, the Franklin Christmas Tree glowed beautiful and bright with a magical light all its own. On the tippy top of the tree appeared a star, shining with the purest light that could be seen for miles around. From the oldest to the youngest, every heart was filled with gratitude.

Soon Christmas came, and guided by the magical light of the Franklin Christmas tree, Saint Nicholas visited Franklin once again. The children woke up on Christmas morning to find all kinds of extraordinary gifts in their stockings. However, the children also knew that, as wonderful as the gifts from Saint Nicholas were, none could compare to the gift of love that shined bright in the town square.

Days later, at the stroke of midnight on New Year's Eve, a new glittering magic pinecone appeared on a lower bough of the Franklin Christmas Tree. Once again, the mayor plucked the pinecone and placed it in the chest of gold. And oh, wonder of wonders! The crystal bottle, with the cork as red as holly berries, suddenly began to fill up again with magical melted snow from the North Pole.

The people smiled at the sight, and with happy hearts they watched as the mayor closed the chest of gold. The treasures within would not be seen again until next All Saints Day.

Festivities continued over the ninth, tenth, and eleventh days of Christmas, and then the people were met with one final, glorious surprise.

On the Twelfth day of Christmas, at the stroke of midnight, the light of the Franklin Christmas Tree began to grow brighter and brighter. The entire tree was ablaze with many different colors. Everyone stopped their dancing and singing to watch this magical marvel.

Suddenly, as if saying farewell to the town, the Franklin Christmas Tree joyfully exploded high into the night sky. A flash of light spread, from horizon to horizon, and then faded, leaving only the moon and stars looking down on the now empty town square.

The people cheered! The people laughed. The people sang. The people danced. The people were grateful.

And so, the magic of the first Franklin Christmas Tree continues because it was created with the Greatest Magic of all. The Magic of Love. Year after year, and Christmas after Christmas, this love lives on in the hearts of the people of Franklin, as family, friends, and neighbors all. They continue to cheer. They continue to laugh. They continue to sing. They continue to dance. And they continue to love until the season comes round again.